The
Magic Butterfly
And The
Flower of Life

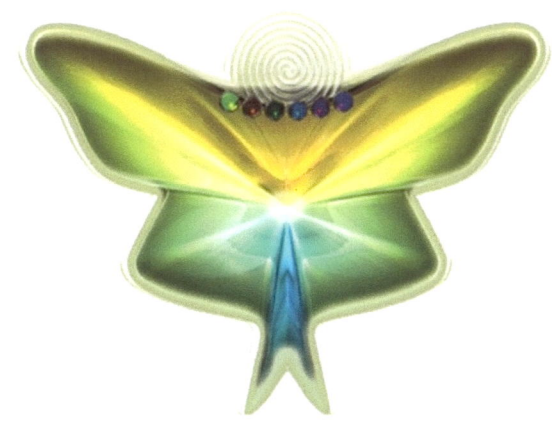

by
A.M. Curiel

Illustrations by
A.M. Curiel and Daniel B. Arroyo

The dedication of this book goes to:

Pamela & Alessandra Rodriguez

Clara Curiel

Adriana Curiel

Alicia Zarraga

Roberto Curiel

Stephanie

Sophia

Alejandro Curiel

Aida Marquez

Diego Falcon

Ana Mesa

Steven Effman

Morela Machado

Luz

Daniel Arroyo

Lori Ann

Judge N 7

James Martucci

And to all of you!

Library of Congress Cataloging-in-Publication Data

Table of Contents

Chapter One

Ark

A long time ago, a massive star died in the center of many galaxies. Then, a black hole appeared and everything nearby—stars, dust clouds, and even light—got trapped and sucked in.

This created a tunnel between two different universes. On the other side, the birth of a new solar system was taking place. Slowly rocky planets began to organize themselves finding their own orbit. Among them one planet stood out. Ark, the newest sphere in this universe, traced its path as the third planet from the sun.

The particles floating around Ark, formed two butterfly shaped rings. The red ring gave the inhabitants the power to LOVE all creatures, while the blue ring gave them the power to BELIEVE in themselves. For quite some time these rings created a lot of happiness on planet Ark.

From the beginning, the only living beings on the planet were vividly colored butterflies. As time went on, these butterflies evolved into human beings.

There was a beautiful Kingdom named Aregon. It was ruled by King Eeman and his beautiful wife Larah. They had a son, Lamed. This boy was their pride and joy. Lamed, unlike the other boys, cared only for his books.

One day, carried away by his curiosity, Lamed asked his father, "Why do I always have to wear this necklace around my neck?"

"My son, that is a special locket. It is the key to open the Flower of Life," King Eeman explained. "The water on planet Ark is our greatest treasure, it is the fountain of life. With that necklace, you will protect it from hate."

Little did they know a spider was peeping in from behind the lamp, and had been listening in on their whole conversation.

Hydrus, the spider, anxiously ran to the laboratory to tell Dolos what he had just heard.

Dolos was King Eeman's brother. Ever since his father had chosen Eeman as King, and not him, Dolos had been angry and resentful. As years passed, Dolos' envy for Eeman turned into hatred, and with that, Ark's worst enemy was born.

Mulling over this unexpected secret, a million ideas began spinning in Dolos' head. He pieced together a peculiar machine while saying, "Hmm, I shall give my nephew Lamed a birthday present he will never forget."

Chapter Two

The Great Tragedy

At last, Lamed's long-awaited 15th birthday had arrived!

King Eeman, and Queen Larah, got up extra early to help decorate the castle courtyard. They wanted everything to be just right for their son's big day.

That morning, Toffler, a very unique fish capable of living in and out of the water, crept into Lamed's room. He shook his wet fins as usual to awaken him, "Pssst. I'm sorry pal, but guess what? There is a huge gift waiting for you outside."

Lamed was snuggled under his covers, but when he heard the work 'gift' he hopped out of bed and eagerly headed for the courtyard.

His jaw dropped as he looked at the huge gift box.
"Who is this gift from?" Lamed asked.

"This is a surprise I made especially for you my dear
nephew," Dolos answered cunningly. "It is a machine that
creates special bubbles. Once they reach a certain height,
they will pop and form one-of-a-kind fireworks show!"

After Lamed's friends arrived, he showed them with pride the gift from his uncle. Immediately, Lamed turned on the machine and minutes later the skies of Ark were completely covered with bright bubbles.

"Look!" Toffler was pulling Lamed's pants desperately, "Those bubbles are kind of scary-looking. Don't you think?"

But Lamed ignored Toffler's concerns and kept playing with his friends.

Relaxing music began to play, and the first dance started around the Merkaba Fountain.

The bubbles suddenly popped over the ocean, and out slid thirsty creatures, capable of swallowing tons of water all at once.

A moment later, the pleasant sound of falling water from the fountain stopped. This caused great alarm throughout the palace, it was the first time the pleasant rhythm of the water falling had gone silent.

"Look!" screamed Toffler with his fins on his head. "The Ray of Light Ocean has almost disappeared."

"You were right, Toffler! I should have listened to you," Lamed was in shock. "Those creatures are drinking all the water."

Immediately the emergency sirens went off, while all the inhabitants began to lose strength.

"Oh no! What is happening?" Lamed exclaimed, rushing to his parents' side.

"I am sorry, my son," King Eeman said sadly. "We just wanted to give you the perfect birthday."

"Please don't leave me… why is everyone dozing off except me?" Lamed asked confused.

King Eeman replied with a weak voice, "We can't live without water, but you are protected because of the locket around your neck. Now go, and find the Flower of Life before it is too late."

Lamed watched in disbelief as everyone collapsed to ground, including his best friend Toffler.

Feeling lonely, he sat underneath the fountain and cried his eyes out.

Suddenly, he saw something familiar. Lamed quickly dried his eyes and focused on a hole inside the crystal star below the fountain. How strange…it is the same shape as my necklace, Lamed thought.

Feeling hopeful, Lamed grabbed the locket and reached out to place it in the hole.

As if by magic, the pyramids around the fountain began to shoot out multicolor rays. It was a spectacular light show!

Immediately, the fountain began to rise revealing a pink misty veil.

Lamed took a few steps forward until he heard an angelic voice, "Dear young one, what brings you here?"

"I need to find the Flower of Life." Lamed's voice was trembling.

"I have what you need, but you will also have to do something on your own. You will need to believe in yourself, otherwise the Flower of Life won't help you," the voice warned.

At that moment, the veil opened and a stunning flower of intense colors was revealed.

Chapter Three

The Magic Caves of Suvat

After walking for hours through the dried up ocean, the flower slowly began to wither. Lamed fell into despair trying to find even a little puddle of water.

"I've heard of your troubles, young boy." An old octopus moved closer to Lamed. "I am Master Ashva."

"Master, I need to find water; otherwise, the flower will die, and with it Ark's hope."

"It would be a miracle for you to find water. The ocean has dried up completely." Master Ashva saw a trace of sadness in Lamed's face. Then he added, "Nevertheless, the Caves of Suvat hide many secrets. It may be possible for you to find water there. Now go, there is not much more time!" Master Ashva advised Lamed.

Without a pause, Lamed thundered off toward the caves. When he reached inside, it became darker and darker until he could no longer see anything.

An icy wind whistled through the cave, his teeth were chattering. He was scared. In that moment, he remembered what the voice told him, "Believe in yourself." Lamed held the locket between his hands and began to speak aloud from the bottom of his heart. "I wish to save planet Ark, I want to save planet Ark, and I will save planet Ark."

Just then, two purple flashes of light shot out of his locket, as if trying to show him something.

Lamed closely followed the beam of light until they stopped on the side of an enormous rock covered in algae.

From the top of the stone, he saw small drops of water trickling down from above. He quickly placed the flower underneath in hope of a miracle.

Lamed could not believe his eyes! With the mere touch of the water, the flower began to grow bigger and bigger, to such a size that it broke through the walls of the cave.

In one magical instant, the small flower turned into a magnificent castle, surrounded by a reef of blooming buds. The entrance was made of hundreds of colorful stained-glass windows that illuminated the castle.

Lamed looked around realizing he was now inside of the huge flower. It was a great room. The walls were made up of thousands of petals, filling up the entire castle with a flowery smell.

Suddenly, there appeared a strong gust of wind from above. The ceiling central lamp opened, releasing hundreds of crystal balls floating downwards in swirling spirals.

As the balls bumped into each other, they created a sound like that of clinking crystal glass.

When they broke, delicate and colorful butterflies came out of them.

Each butterfly had a letter on its back. They organized by color and started forming words above a cocoon beginning with UNDERSTANDING, TOLERANCE, RESPECT, FORGIVENESS, HUMILITY, AND KINDNESS.

Seconds later, the cocoon opened, and a beautiful butterfly girl came out.

"Who are you?" Lamed could not believe his eyes. She smiled softly, "I am Aletheia, the Magic Butterfly." She stood up and with a firm voice, she sang:

"Doubt sees the obstacle,
Believing is the way,
When both are united
Come to save the day."

As soon as she had spoken, sparkling water gushed up from the ground, filling back up the Ray of Light Ocean again!

Chapter Four

The Unexpected

Unexpectedly, Lamed and the Magic Butterfly heard a strange noise. They ran outside the castle, and to their great shock, Hydrus had covered the entire castle with a huge web.

"Uncle, what are you doing with that creepy spider?" Lamed asked.

"Foolish boy," Dolos said gruffly. "Clearly, you don't know me at all. When your grandfather was alive, he chose your father as king and not me. I would have been a much better king than your father."

"Uncle! How can you?" Lamed exclaimed. "And you wonder why you weren't the chosen prince?"

Dolos did not respond, but only glared at his nephew as the spider crept closer.

The Magic Butterfly was quick to react. She swooped up Lamed by the waist and fled the castle.

The Magic Butterfly carefully released Lamed at the top of the algae rock.

What they didn't know was that the surface where they stood wasn't an algae covered rock at all—it was the belly of a sleeping starfish that was about to wake up.

"Oh no! The floor is moving," Lamed was trying to keep his balance so as not to fall.

"What is happening? Help!" screamed Aletheia. "I feel like I am getting swallowed."

Lamed tried to help her, but his effort was useless.

The starfish trapped them inside his transparent membranes and whisked through the water.

"Where are we going?" Aletheia asked.

"I don't know, but I have never seen the bottom of the ocean so close." Lamed was delighted.

Moments later, they entered an air pocket in the underwater cave. Safe now, the starfish released them. They found themselves before a vaulted entrance, as colorful as a rainbow.

Suddenly they heard a loud booming laugh. It was so contagious that they could not contain their own laughter.

"Do you hear all that noise? And just who can it be? Let's sneak down the hall," said Lamed.

To their surprise, they saw an unusual looking animal, similar to an octopus.

"Who are you?" Aletheia asked.

The animal greeted them in his high-spirited way. "Welcome, what a surprise! I haven't had visitors since… well never. Anyway, my name is Rakie," he said, pronouncing each word with a separate mouth.

"Hi…" responded Lamed as he stared at Rakie's multiple eyes, "Would you mind telling me why you laugh so much?"

Rakie responded, "Well son, isn't it obvious? Laughter is the music of the heart! You see, these small eyes around me only show me the past and the future, but that did not make me happy. Only when I started to use my large main eye to see the present did I find true happiness."

Suddenly, the conversation was interrupted by a bright light that almost blinded them.

"Look! The pyramid is lighting up," Rakie exclaimed. "The six cornerstones have awakened. Hmm… something important must be happening for them to open the multidimensional gate."

"Gate? What do you mean?" Lamed asked confused.

"Don't worry my friend, just go through the door, and you'll see," Rakie responded with delight.

Chapter Five

The Big Surprise

Since the door was so small, only Lamed and Magic Butterfly could fit in.

On the other side, they found themselves inside a huge dome. As they moved about, their movements became slower, as if they were not allowed to be in a hurry.

"What is happening? I am moving like a sloth stuck in molasses." Lamed was fighting to speed up his movements.

"There is no time here, Lamed," Aletheia replied slowly. "This is the infinite dimension where everything is possible."

At the back of the dome was a pink arch with twelve floating bubbles of different sizes. As the two got closer, they touched the bubbles—each one created its own musical sound.

After many tries, Aletheia accidentally touched all twelve balls at the same time with her wings. Surprisingly, six strong lights shot out from the arch pointing in the direction of the gigantic petals resting on the ground.

The petals began to move, causing the flower bulb located in the middle to open. Inside was a stunning crystal butterfly, covered with shimmering colors.

"What is that?" asked Lamed.

"It is the Trans-Butterfly. It is used to transform hate into love," the Magic Butterfly responded while the Trans-Butterfly flew to her belt.

"But how?"

"In the same way darkness disappears when light appears, is how hate disappears when love appears."

"How sweet… and you expect to save Ark with that thing," a creepy voice interrupted them sarcastically.

Dolos appeared out of nowhere. He grabbed the Trans-Butterfly from Aletheia's belt while Hydrus trapped them in a huge spider web. They were helpless.

Dolos made several attempts to break the Trans-Butterfly, but before he could destroy it, a beautiful blue dolphin jumped out of the water. It was Sparkle! A dolphin that could swim, fly, and walk. He hit Dolos from behind, causing him to release the Trans-Butterfly.

Aletheia quickly took the Trans-Butterfly and flung it
toward Dolos, creating a magnetic field around him, as
she sang:

> "My love goes with you,
> Like a gentle, flying dove –
> Releasing all your hatred
> And turning it into love."

Immediately Dolos began to transform into a kind and compassionate person. But, in her attempt to transform Hydrus as well, she accidently broke one of the walls of the dome with the Trans-Butterfly. With a rush of water, the place began to flood.

"Quickly!" shouted Lamed. "We must break the chains that tie the dome to the bottom of the ocean."

With everyone's help, they were able to cut the chains. The dome rose fast to the surface creating an undercurrent that pulled everyone up with it.

Chapter Six

The Unimaginable Event

When the dome reached the surface, it split in half, like an oyster.

Lamed saw Dolos and Hydrus floating inside the cocoons, while Sparkle swam about.

Suddenly, Toffler jumped out of the water. "Finally, I found you my friend." He helped Lamed get to the shore.

But their happy reunion was cut short by the body of the Magic Butterfly floating motionless in the water.

"Aletheia!" Lamed shouted. He swam toward her and carried her body over to the flower bulb.

He tried to wake her up, but her heart was no longer beating. Lamed clutched his chest, feeling his own heart shatter.

Minutes later, the Trans-Butterfly left Aletheia's belt.

THE SIX ELEMENTS MUST BE CONVINCED OF YOUR PURE EMOTIONS, FOR THEM TO BRING BACK THE MOST BELOVED OF ALL

In the midst of their sadness, the Trans-Butterfly flew toward Lamed, moving its wings so softly that it resembled an angel. Flashes of light full of energy came out, projecting a hologram, "The six elements must be convinced of your pure emotions, for them to bring back the most beloved of all."

Immediately Sparkle jumped, "I know, I know! The gigantic petals are the six elements! I have lived with them for a while, and believe me they are sooo sensitive," he said rolling his eyes. "They can perceive the smallest of feelings if anyone sits upon them."

Quickly, Lamed, Sparkle, Toffler, Dolos, and Hydrus climbed onto the petals. But they were only five, and one more was needed.

For a moment they were discouraged, but their hope returned when they saw a gigantic eye coming out of the water.

"Hello all—I have come to the rescue!" exclaimed Rakie, sitting on the orange petal.

The petals grew happy to perceive the lovely and honest feelings from all of them. Immediately, the flower bulb rose spinning in the air. As it gained speed, it began to look like a tornado.

The performance lasted a couple of seconds, and soon enough the spinning stopped.

Then something amazing happened. At that moment, the flower bulb opened slowly, and a human shape approached through the fog.

Everyone was ecstatic—especially Lamed—when
they realized it was the Magic Butterfly. She was dressed
in a beautiful pink dress with colorful crystals flowing
down her skirt.

The castle came to life with rejoicing. The Magic Butterfly sent thousands of butterflies to invite all the inhabitants to her castle, especially the King and Queen.

Ice butterflies froze the surface. At the same time, the wind chimes hanging on the windows began to play enchanting notes as the butterflies flew by.

Lamed asked the Magic Butterfly to dance with him. His heart beat rapidly as they danced together.

"Ah," exclaimed Toffler. "My friend is feeling something different."

"What is that?" asked Sparkle.

"Romantic love, my dear friend."

They all celebrated with a big feast and danced until dawn. As long as the Magic Butterfly existed, the planet would always be safe from hate.

"Love is to understand
without reservation
that we are in perfect unity
with all existence."

Only Our Love Will Live

Verse 1
In this land where we live
We share the same life
Flows like the waters
Shines like our light

Accept it within you
Fall from hate
Be the light of today
Understand our faith

Chorus
Only our love will live
Only our love will save us

Verse 2
The Flower of Life
Appears so magically
Glowing with colors
In the sky for all to see

Love will be reborn
Understanding is key
Tolerance, **Respect**,
Forgiveness, **Humility**,
Fills us with **Goodness**
And set us free

Chorus 2
Only our love will live
Only our love will save us

Bridge
Forgiveness